The Hopeful Little Leopard

Written by Jane Monmouth
Illustrations by Beverly Branch

Published by The Reader's Digest Association Limited
London • New York • Sydney • Montreal

‘Mum’s been gone a long time,’ Lenny said anxiously to his brother, Larry.

Their mother had left their cave the day before to search for something to eat. The weather was hot and food was hard to find.

‘I’m sure she’ll be back any time now,’ said Larry, trying to comfort his brother.

But Lenny still looked unhappy.

At last, their mother returned. 'I'm sorry,' she said. 'It's so hot. I had to travel a long way from home to find food.'

Mother Leopard had only managed to bring back a few fish and some fruit, which the hungry cubs ate eagerly.

'I told you she'd be back!' said Larry to his brother as they snuggled with their mother.

Soon afterwards, the weather changed completely and the rainy season arrived.

'I must find some more food for us,' said Mother Leopard, giving both cubs a kiss. 'I won't be gone long. Do be careful and stay close to home.'

The two brothers sat quietly watching the rain. Lenny was the first to speak. 'What if she doesn't come back?' he asked his brother anxiously.

'Don't be such a worrier', said Larry. She's only been gone an hour.'

'I wish I could be more like you,' said Lenny. 'You're always so full of hope.'

Larry grinned. 'Come on,' he said, jumping up. 'Let's go out and play in the rain.'

Lenny followed his brother cautiously outside the cave. The rain pounded down on them, and in minutes they were both drenched.

'Isn't this fun?' shouted Larry.

Then suddenly–WHOOSH! A huge gush of water from an overflowing stream swept the two little cubs off their feet and into the water.

Far downstream, the rush of water finally slowed down and they were able to climb onto a rocky shore.

Lenny looked around. ‘Where are we?’ he asked his brother nervously.

Larry looked around, too. ‘I don’t know,’ he sighed. He felt very tearful. ‘I can’t see how we’ll ever get back up that mountain, and it’s all my fault.’

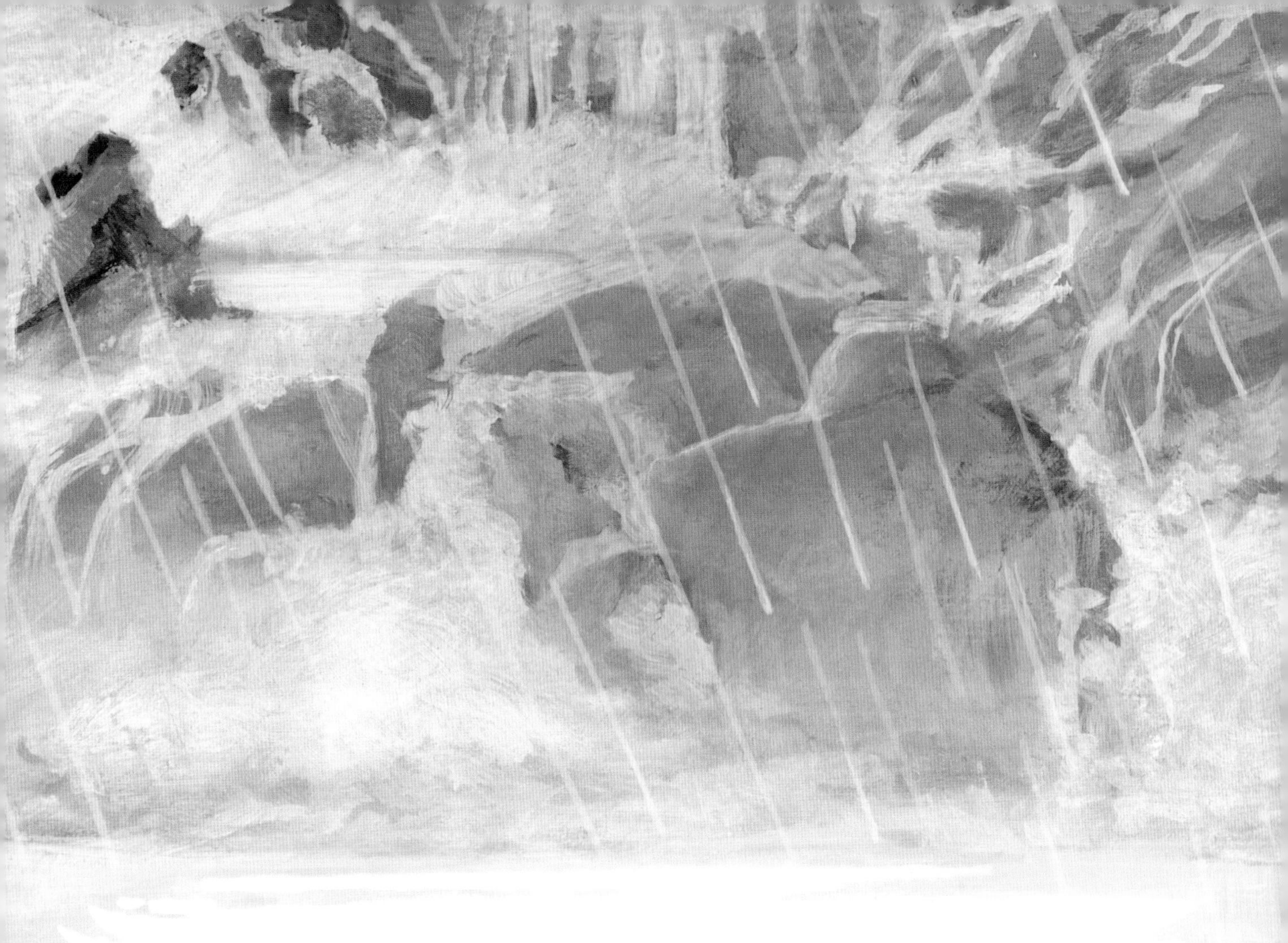

Lenny looked at his brother in surprise. 'Larry,' he said, giving his brother a reassuring pat. 'Don't give up so soon. You're always the brave one. We mustn't lose hope. Come on. The rain is stopping. We have to climb back up the mountain or Mum will wonder where we are and be very worried when she gets back.'

Larry smiled at his brother. 'Okay,' he said, feeling better. 'Let's have a go.'

The two cubs struggled up the mountain with Larry leading the way.

'Come on, Lenny,' panted Larry, who was beginning to feel much more hopeful. 'I'm sure we'll see the cave any minute now.'

Lenny was too tired to talk, but he nodded his head bravely and kept walking.

And then Lenny noticed a familiar tree, and then another, and another.

'There's the cave!' shouted Larry, as he spotted their home.

The two cubs used every bit of strength they had left to scamper to the cave's opening.

And there, inside, was …

… Mother Leopard.

'Mum!' shouted Lenny, tumbling into his mother's arms. Larry did the same.

'Oh, my little cubs,' said their mother, kissing them both. 'I was so afraid you were lost, but I didn't lose hope that you would come back.'

'We tried not to lose hope either,' said Larry, smiling at his brother.

As the two cubs ate the food their mother had brought back, the sun came out from behind the clouds for the first time in many days. Lenny looked outside and said happily, ‘Let’s hope the weather stays this nice.’

‘Yes,’ agreed Larry. ‘Let’s hope.’

All about ... LEOPARDS

BIG PUSSYCATS

Leopards are members of the cat family. They are related to house cats, but they are wild animals that live in Asia and Africa.

SUPER FIT

Leopards are fast runners, reaching speeds of 40 miles per hour. They also jump, swim and climb trees. They have good hearing and excellent eyesight which helps them to find prey.

FACT FILE

GREAT TAILS

Leopards grow to be about 2 metres long from the nose to the tip of the tail. Their tails help them to balance.

Did you know?

CUNNING DISGUISE

A leopard's furry coat is usually yellow or brown with black spots. The spots help the leopard to blend into the surroundings and remain hidden.

BLACK BEASTS

Some leopards are born with an all-black coat. They are called black panthers and have spots, but you usually can't see them.

NIGHT HUNTERS

Leopards are nocturnal animals which means they are most active at night, though they may hunt in daylight, too.

The Hopeful Little Leopard is a Little Animal Adventures book
published by Reader's Digest Young Families, Inc.
by arrangement with Éditions Nathan, Paris, France

Written by Jane Monmouth
Illustrations by Beverly Branch
Notebook artwork © Paul Bommer

This edition was adapted and published in 2008 by
The Reader's Digest Association Limited
11 Westferry Circus, Canary Wharf, London E14 4HE

Printed in China

Book code: 637-017 UP0000-1
ISBN: 978 0 276 44349 7
Oracle code: 501800105H.00.24